The Bear and the Piano

To Katie and Ben.
—D.L.

First published in Great Britain in 2015 by Frances Lincoln Children's Books
This first paperback edition published in Great Britain in 2016 by Frances Lincoln Children's Books,
74-77 White Lion Street, London N1 9PF
QuartoKnows.com
Visit our blogs at QuartoKnows.com

Text and illustrations copyright © David Litchfield 2015

The right of David Litchfield to be identified as the author and illustrator
of this work has been asserted by him in accordance with the
Copyright, Designs and Patents Act, 1988 (United Kingdom).

A catalogue record for this book is available from the British Library.

ISBN 978-1-84780-718-2

Illustrated digitally

Designed by Andrew Watson • Edited by Katie Cotton

Printed in Italy by L.E.G.O. S.p.A.

3 5 7 9 8 6 4

The Bear and the Piano

David Litchfield

Frances Lincoln
Children's Books

One day in the forest, a young bear cub
found something he'd never seen before.

"What could this strange thing be?" he thought.
Shyly, he touched it with his stubby paws.

"PLONK!"

The strange thing made an
awful sound.

So, the bear left.

But the next day he came back,

and the day after that too.

And for days and weeks and months and years,

until eventually…

The sounds that came from the strange thing
were beautiful, and the bear had grown
big and strong and grizzly.

When the bear played, he felt so happy.

The sound took him away from the forest,

and he dreamed of strange and wonderful lands.

It wasn't long before the other bears
in the forest were drawn to the clearing.

Every night, a crowd gathered to listen
to the magical melodies coming from
the bear and the strange thing.

Then, one night, a girl and her father came across the clearing.

They told the bear that the strange thing was a piano and the sounds it made were music.

"Come to the city with us," they said. "There is lots of music there. You can play grand pianos in front of hundreds of people and hear sounds so beautiful they will make your fur stand on end."

The bear knew that if he left the forest, the other bears would miss him very much.

But he longed to explore the world beyond the woods, to hear more wonderful music and play better than ever before.

And before long…

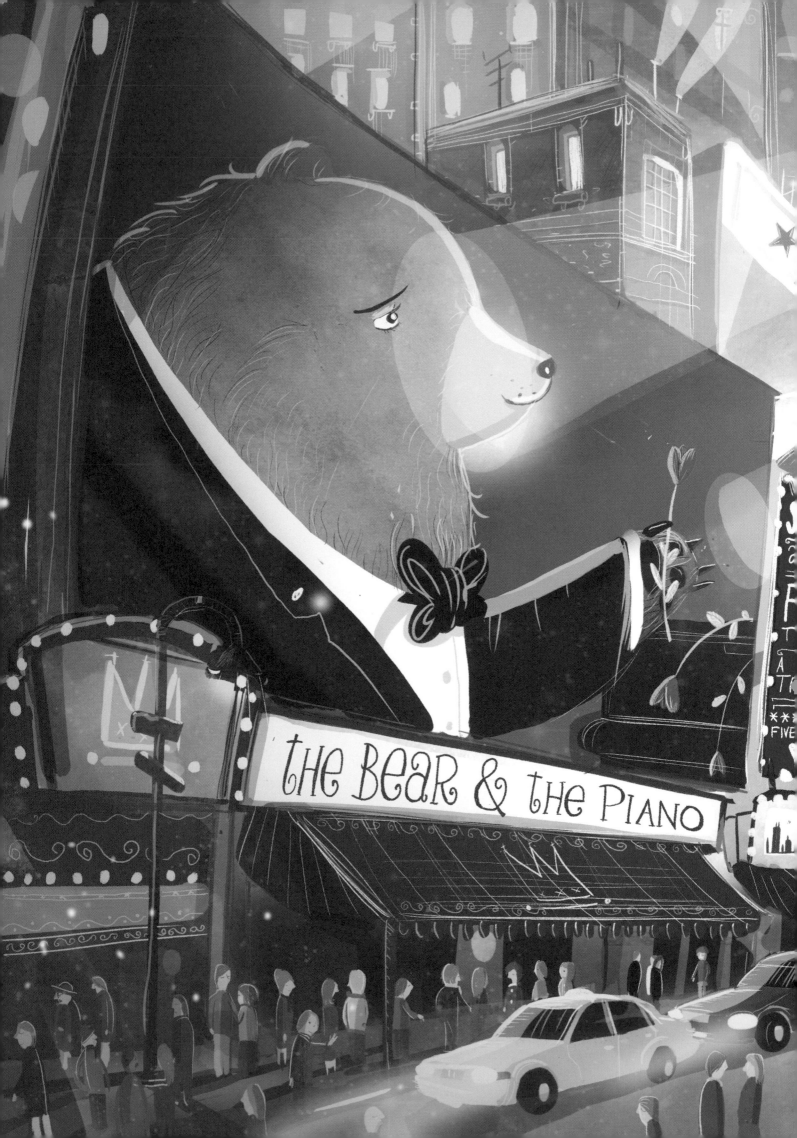

The bear's name was up in
big, bright lights in the big, bright city.

He played sold-out concerts

in giant theatres.

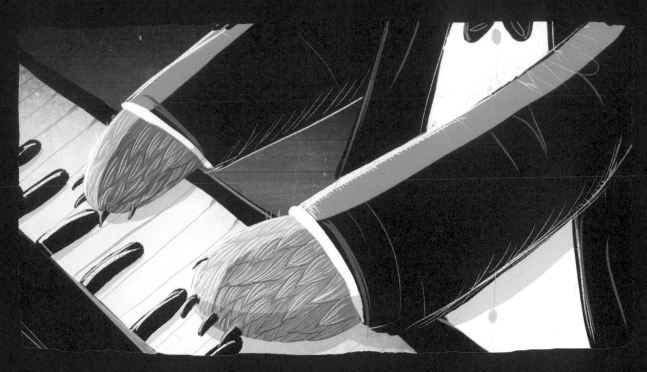

Every night, he performed

with such passion

and such grace,

to wild applause

and standing ovations

and huge admiration.

The bear recorded albums that went platinum.
He was interviewed for magazines.

He won awards.
He met new people everyday
and created headlines everywhere he went.

PIANO PLAYING BEAR IS A REAL SMASH!

PAWS FOR THOUGHT!

BEAR'S WORLD TOUR SELLS OUT!

the Bear & the Piano

The city was everything he had hoped it would be.

But deep down, something tugged at the bear's heart.

He had fame and awards and all the music in the world,
but he missed the forest.

He missed his old friends.

He missed his home.

So the bear decided to go back.
He speedily crossed the river…

and excitedly bounded into the forest. He couldn't
wait to tell his friends about his time in the city.

But when the bear reached the
familiar clearing it was empty.

No piano, no bears, no anything.

The bear started to worry that his friends
had forgotten him, or that they were
angry that he had left them behind.

Then a friend stepped into the clearing.
"Hello!" cried the bear. "I'm back. I've missed
you so much!"

Without saying a word, the grey bear ran back into the forest.
"Wait!" called the bear. "I'm sorry I left. Please stop!"
But his friend just kept running.

The bear stumbled after him, moving deeper and
deeper into the forest,

until he saw something that made his fur stand on end.

For the bear had not been forgotten.
His friends weren't angry, but proud.

The bear realised that no matter where he went, or what he did,
they would always be there, watching from afar.

They had even kept the piano safe
in the shade, ready for his return.

So after the bear had told his
friends about his life in the city,
and the many concerts he had played,
he sat down to play once more.

This time, for the most
important audience of all.

David Litchfield first began drawing when he was very young. His illustration heroes and biggest influences are Albert Uderzo, Sylvain Chomet, Jon Klassen and Shaun Tan. He creates his unique, atmospheric artwork using a variety of traditional techniques, assembling the different elements together in Photoshop to create large-scale, dramatic scenes. *The Bear and the Piano*, David's first picture book, was inspired by his love of music, forests and The White Stripes' song, 'Little Room'.